ELMER ON STILTS

For Oscar and Jo

A RED FOX BOOK : 0 09 929671 3

First published in Great Britain by Andersen Press Ltd 1993
Red Fox edition published 1994

10

copyright © David McKee 1993

The right of David McKee to be identified as the author and illustrator of this
work has been asserted in accordance with the Copyright, Designs and Patents Act 1988

Red Fox Books are published by Random House Children's Books,
61-63 Uxbridge Road, London W5 5SA,
a division of The Random House Group Ltd,
in Australia by Random House Australia (Pty) Ltd,
20 Alfred Street, Milsons Point, Sydney, NSW 2061, Australia
in New Zealand by Random House New Zealand Ltd,
18 Poland Road, Glenfield, Auckland 10, New Zealand
and in South Africa by Random House (Pty) Ltd,
Endulini, 5A Jubilee Road, Parktown 2193, South Africa

THE RANDOM HOUSE GROUP Limited Reg No. 954009
www.kidsatrandomhouse.co.uk

A CIP catalogue record for this book is available from the British Library.

Printed in Singapore

ELMER ON STILTS

David McKee

Red Fox

One morning, Elmer, the patchwork elephant, met some of his friends. They were looking very worried.

"Oh dear, Elmer," they said. "Those awful elephant hunters are coming. What can we do to escape them?"

"Hmmmm!" said Elmer. "Let me have a think. I'm sure I can come up with something."

Elmer went for a thinking walk. He was thinking about how hunters look for elephant footprints and follow them until they find the elephants when suddenly a voice said,

"Look out, Elmer. Watch where you're going." A very tall giraffe was speaking to him.

"Sorry," said Elmer. "I didn't see you up there. But you've just given me a very good idea," and he hurried off to find the other elephants.

"I've an idea," said Elmer to the others. "Let's walk around on stilts."

"This is no time for jokes, Elmer," said an elephant. "The hunters are coming."

"I'm serious," said Elmer. "Hunters look for us by following our footprints. They'd never look up and see us."

The elephants thought that Elmer's idea was a good one and were soon hard at work. Some made stilts from very strong wood.

Other elephants brought tree trunks and made a ramp
that the elephants could walk up to get onto the stilts.

Elmer went first. He walked up the ramp, and using his front legs to hold on he put his back legs onto the stilts. "It's easy," he called. "My trunk helps me to keep my balance."

Unfortunately, because Elmer was so heavy the stilts immediately sank into the ground.

"Oh no," groaned the elephants. "It won't work."

"I know," said Elmer. "If we put flat pieces of wood on the bottom of the poles, the stilts won't sink into the ground."

"Then if we colour the stilts green," continued
Elmer, "the hunters will think they are plants.
We can shape the flat bits like monsters' feet.
If we put them on backwards, as we walk it will
look like a monsters' trail, but going in the
opposite direction. The hunters will follow the
footprints away from us to try and find the
monsters."

It wasn't long before the elephants were walking on stilts leaving a trail of prints pointing away from them.

"The more the hunters look, the further they will get away from us," chuckled Elmer.

There was one thing, however, that Elmer had forgotten. Elephant hunters are cowards. When they saw the footprints, the hunters all said the same thing.

"Oh no, monsters!" Then, shaking with fear, they hurried off in the opposite direction – towards the elephants and . . .

. . . **CRASH!**
They didn't notice the stilts and bumped right into them.

The elephants fell off, but, instead of falling onto the hard ground, they fell onto the soft, round, fat hunters.

One by one, Elmer and the elephants got up and walked away. "Dear, oh dear," they said.

It was a long time before the hunters managed to crawl away, moaning. They would never come back.

"Hurrah for Elmer," shouted the elephants. "His idea saved us. Now we don't need the stilts any more."

"We don't NEED them," smiled Elmer. "But we could have some fun on them." And that's exactly what they did.

Some bestselling Red Fox picture books